RETURN

Aaron Becker

WALKER BOOKS
AND SUBSIDIARIES
LONDON • BOSTON • SYDNEY • AUCKLAND

For my parents

Special thanks to Natalie Moss for her assistance with the petroglyph design in this book, and to *mis compañeros de erranT* in Granada, Spain, for opening their doors to an artist from far away.

First published 2016 by Walker Books Ltd
87 Vauxhall Walk, London SE11 5HJ

10 9 8 7 6 5 4 3

Printed in China

British Library Cataloguing in Publication Data: a catalogue record for this book is available from the British Library

ISBN 978-1-4063-6843-7

www.walker.co.uk

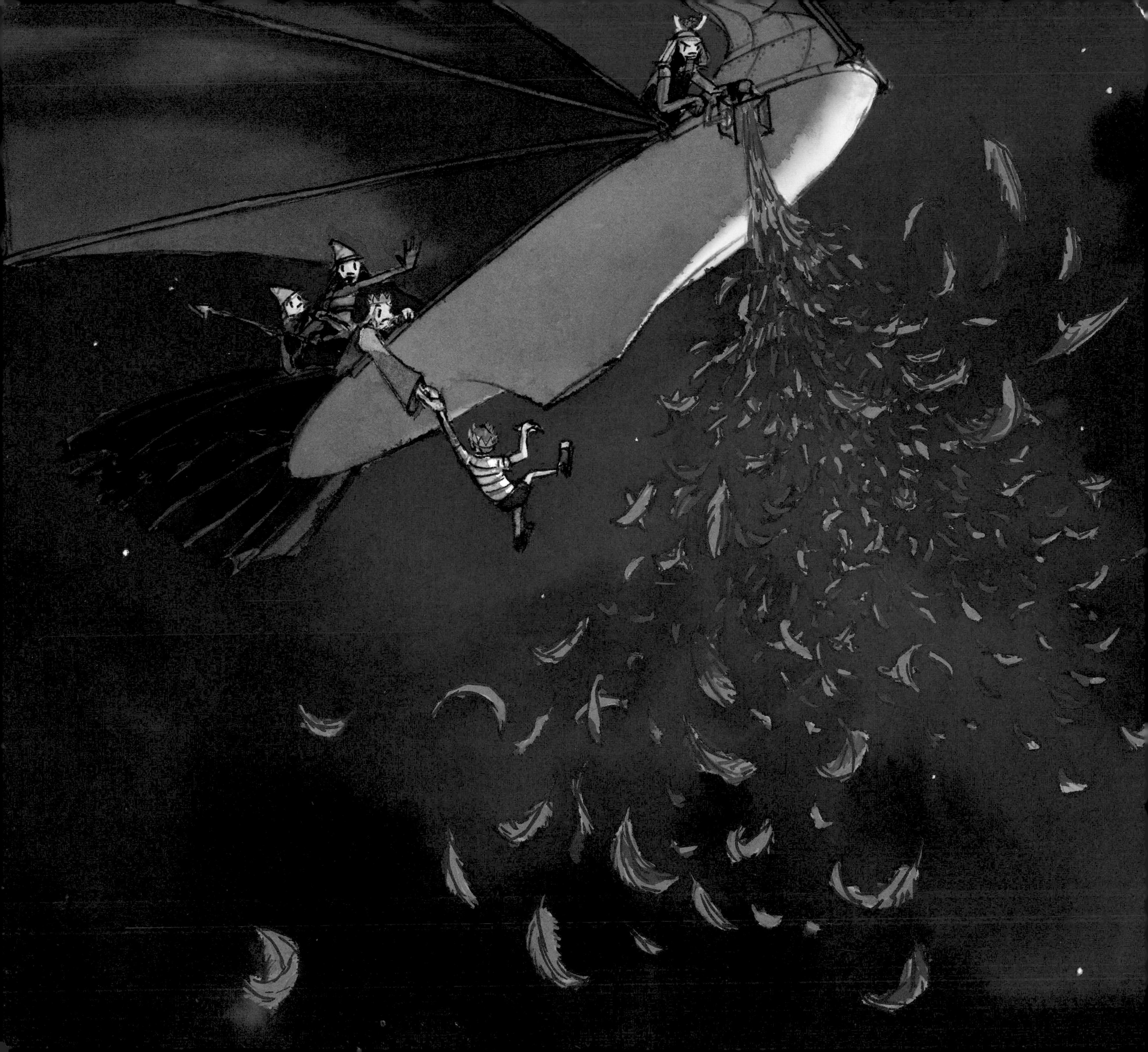